so many days

by ALISON McGHEE

with illustrations by TAEEUN YOO

ATHENEUM
BOOKS FOR YOUNG READERS
New York London Toronto Sydney

So many doors in all your days,
so much to wonder about.

Who will you be and where will you go?
And how will you know?

Words will open your heart
and kindness will open your soul.

So many doors in all your days,
so much to wonder about.

Air you breathe holds the breath of all things.

You are hope that wants to take wing.
You are stronger than you know.

Words will open your heart
and kindness will open your soul.

Air you breathe holds the breath of all things.

You are hope that wants to take wing.
You are stronger than you know.

So many doors in all your days,
so much to wonder about.

Who will you be and where will you go?
And how will you know?

Wind will come before a storm

and snow will silence all sound.

You are a star trailing fire at night.
You are a bird urgent for flight.

You are braver than you know.

So many doors
in all your days,
so much to
wonder about.

Who will you be
and where will you go?

And how
will you know?

A kite will spiral high in the sky,
wanting, like you, to be free.

You are the beat of the sun at noon.
You are the tug and the push
of the moon.

You are wilder than you know.

So many doors in all your days,
so much to wonder about.

Who will you be and where will you go?
And how will you know?

Sometimes you won't.

Mountains and ocean and prairie and tree,
rain on a river that runs to the sea.

You are earth that hungers for sun.
You are song that longs to be sung.

You are loved more than you know.

To Anne Buchanan
—A. M.

To my father, Leejin Yoo,
and mother, Junghyun Sung,
who always trust me
and let me explore
so many doors in my life . . .
with love
—T. Y.

ATHENEUM BOOKS FOR YOUNG READERS
An imprint of Simon & Schuster Children's
Publishing Division
1230 Avenue of the Americas
New York, New York 10020
ATHENEUM BOOKS FOR YOUNG READERS is a registered
trademark of Simon & Schuster, Inc.
For information about special discounts for bulk purchases,
please contact Simon & Schuster Special Sales at
1-866-506-1949 or business@simonandschuster.com.
The Simon & Schuster Speakers Bureau can bring
authors to your live event. For more information or to
book an event, contact the Simon & Schuster Speakers
Bureau at 1-866-248-3049 or visit our website at
www.simonspeakers.com.
Book design by Ann Bobco
The text for this book is set in Century Gothic.
The illustrations for this book are rendered as linocuts
and then manipulated digitally.
Manufactured in China
First Edition
1009 PXA
10 9 8 7 6 5 4 3 2 1
Library of Congress Cataloging-in-Publication Data
McGhee, Alison, 1960–
So many days / Alison McGhee ;
illustrated by Taeeun Yoo.—1st ed.
p. cm.
Summary: Through rhythmic text, a parent reflects on
the options and opportunities possible in a beloved
child's future.
ISBN 978-1-4169-5857-4
[1. Parent and child—Fiction.] I. Yoo, Taeeun, ill. II. Title.
PZ7.M4784675So 2010
[E]—dc22   2008038300